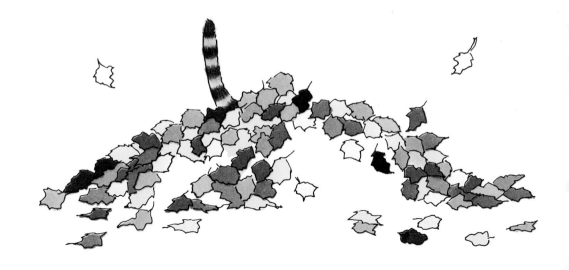

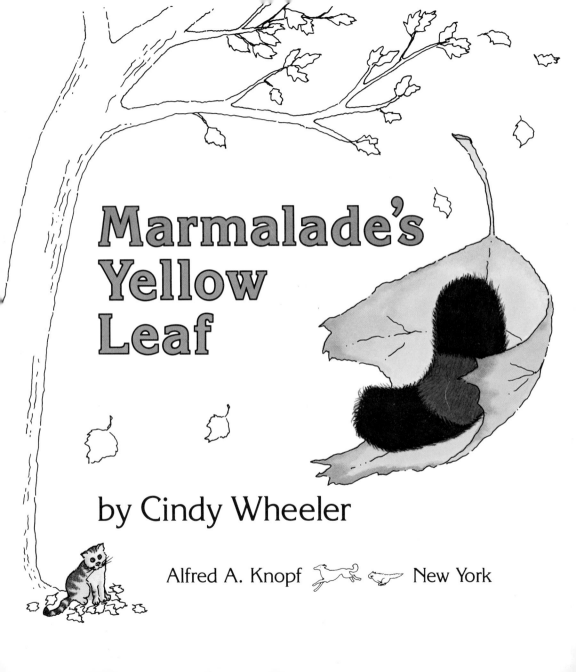

# Marmalade's Yellow Leaf

## by Cindy Wheeler

Alfred A. Knopf · New York

*This is a Borzoi Book published by Alfred A. Knopf, Inc.*

All rights reserved under International and Pan-American Copyright Conventions.
Published in the United States by Alfred A. Knopf, Inc., New York,
and simultaneously in Canada by Random House of Canada Limited, Toronto.
Distributed by Random House, Inc., New York.
Manufactured in the United States of America
2   4   6   8   10   9   7   5   3   1

Library of Congress Cataloging in Publication Data
Wheeler, Cindy. Marmalade's yellow leaf.
*Summary*: Marmalade, a cat, causes a commotion when he tries
to retrieve a particular yellow leaf.
[1. Cats—Fiction. 2. Autumn—Fiction] I. Title.
PZ7.W5593Mas 1982   [E]   81-20793
ISBN 0-394-85024-6   AACR2   ISBN 0-394-95024-0 (lib. bdg.)

Summer is over.

Robin is going south.

Red and yellow leaves are everywhere.

Marmalade chases a yellow leaf.

It is moving!

What's this?

It got away.

Where did it go?

Marmalade doesn't want the woolly worm.

Where did that leaf go?

There it is!

Look out, Marmalade!

Got it!

Cindy Wheeler grew up in Alabama, Virginia, and North Carolina. After receiving a B.F.A. degree from Auburn University, Ms. Wheeler worked for a bookseller and for a publisher. Now she devotes full time to writing and illustrating children's books.

Ms. Wheeler lives in Garrison, New York, with her husband and one black cat.